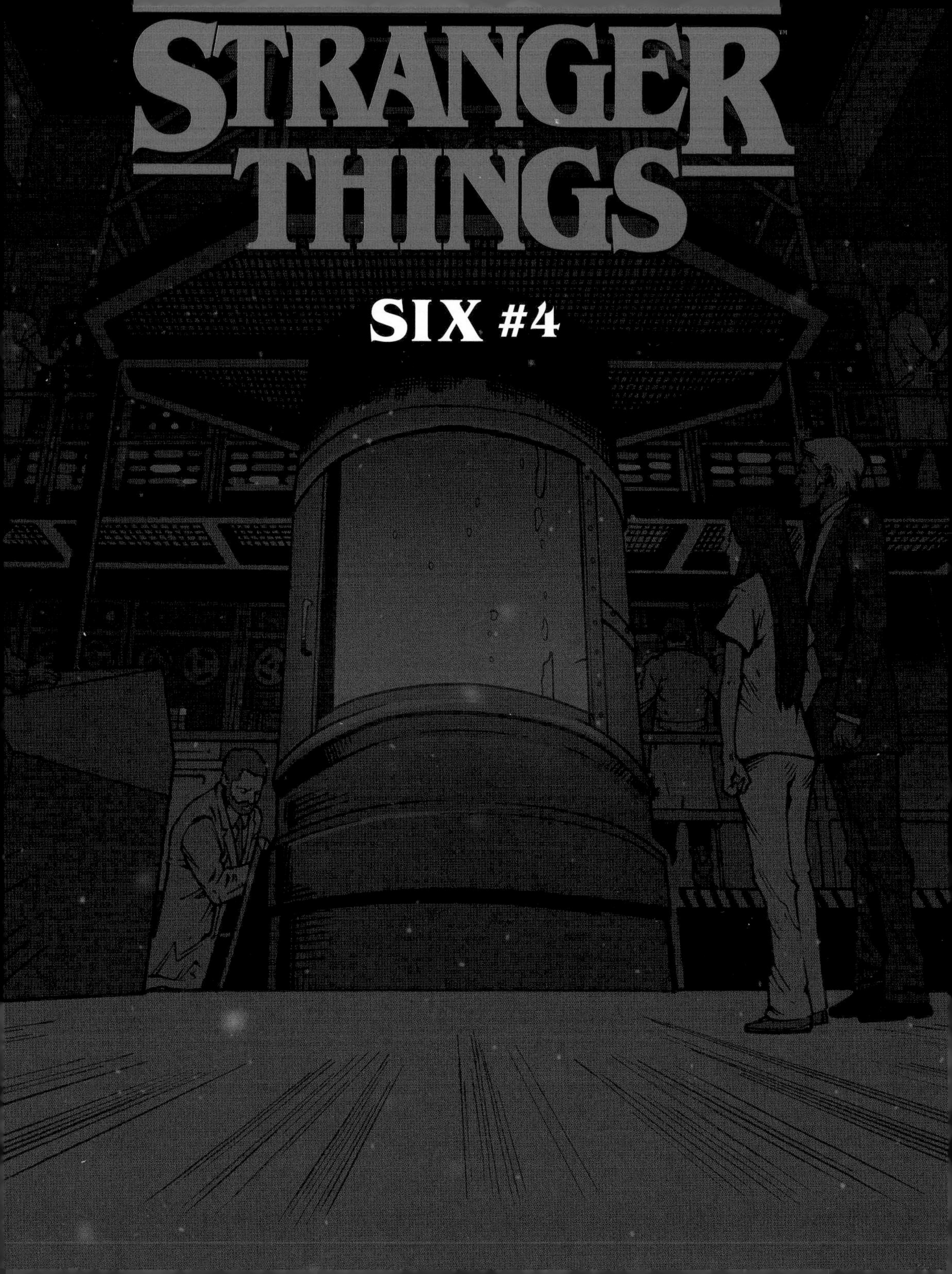
STRANGER THINGS
SIX #4

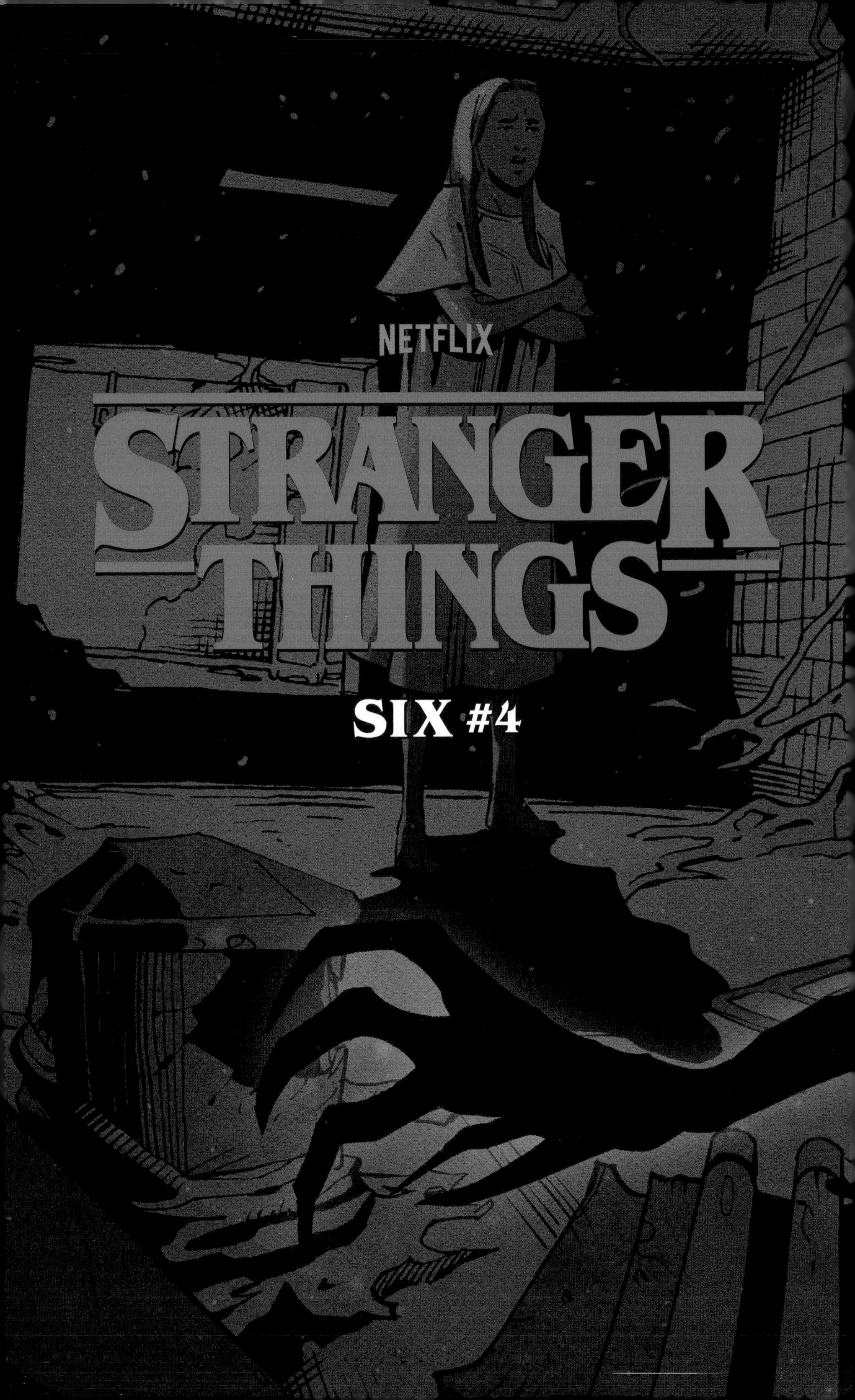
NETFLIX
STRANGER THINGS
SIX #4

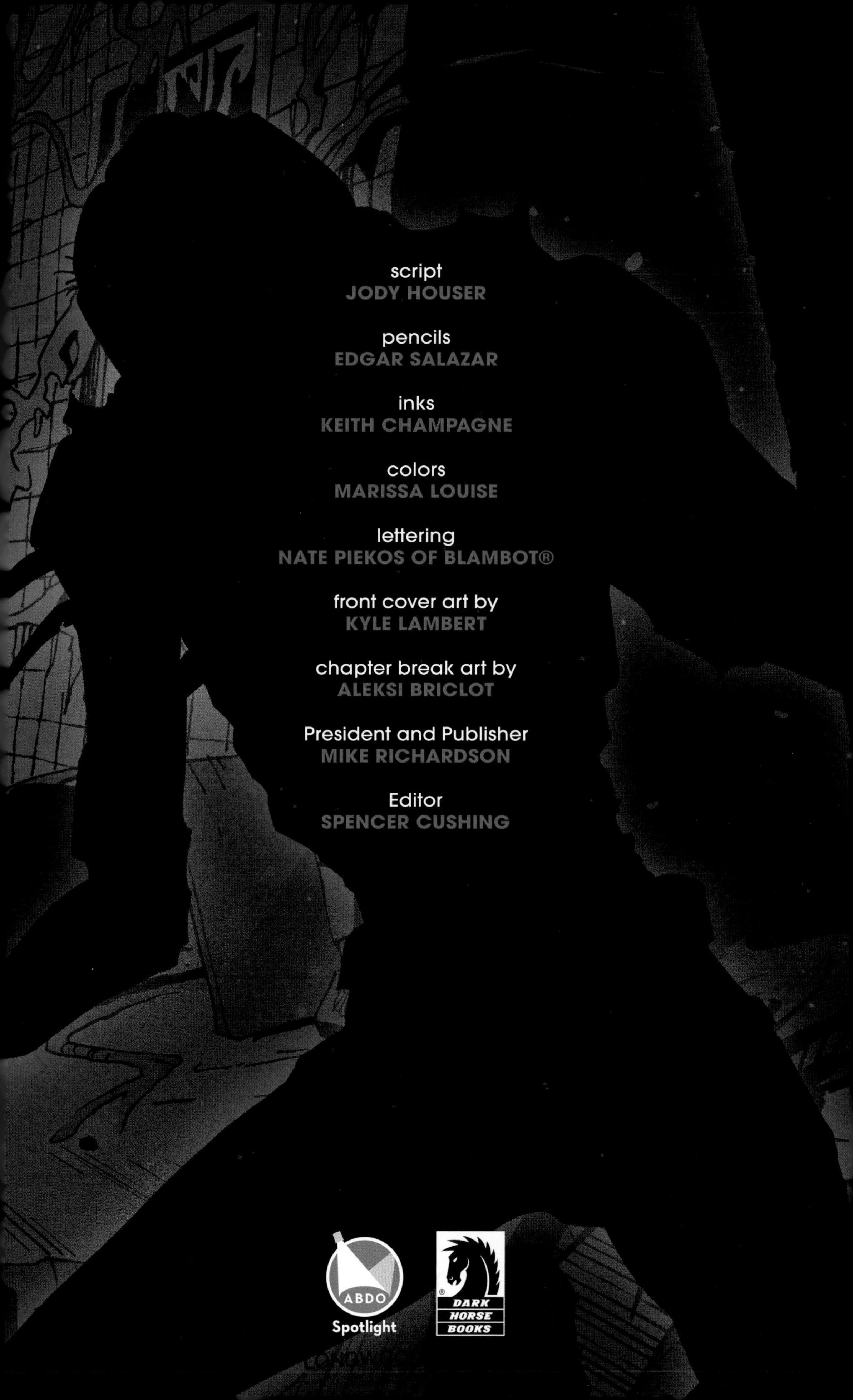

script
JODY HOUSER

pencils
EDGAR SALAZAR

inks
KEITH CHAMPAGNE

colors
MARISSA LOUISE

lettering
NATE PIEKOS OF BLAMBOT®

front cover art by
KYLE LAMBERT

chapter break art by
ALEKSI BRICLOT

President and Publisher
MIKE RICHARDSON

Editor
SPENCER CUSHING

ABDO Spotlight

DARK HORSE BOOKS

ABDOBOOKS.COM

Reinforced library bound edition published in 2020 by Spotlight, a division of ABDO, PO Box 398166, Minneapolis, Minnesota 55439. Spotlight produces high-quality reinforced library bound editions for schools and libraries.
Published by agreement with Dark Horse Comics.

Printed in the United States of America, North Mankato, Minnesota.
092019
012020

THIS BOOK CONTAINS
RECYCLED MATERIALS

NETFLIX
OFFICIAL MERCHANDISE
©NETFLIX

Library of Congress Control Number: 2019942387

Publisher's Cataloging-in-Publication Data

Names: Houser, Jody, author. | Salazar, Edgar; Champagne, Keith; Louise, Marissa; Piekos, Nate, illustrators.
Title: Six / by Jody Houser; illustrated by Edgar Salazar; Keith Champagne; Marissa Louise; Nate Piekos.
Description: Minneapolis, Minnesota : Spotlight, 2020 | Series: Stranger things
Summary: A teenage girl with precognitive abilities ends up as the pawn of a government agency that wants to harness her powers for its own ends.
Identifiers: ISBN 9781532144400 (#1, lib. bdg.) | ISBN 9781532144417 (#2, lib. bdg.) | ISBN 9781532144424 (#3, lib. bdg.) | ISBN 9781532144431 (#4, lib. bdg.)
Subjects: LCSH: Stranger things (Television program)--Juvenile fiction. | Science fiction television programs--Juvenile fiction. | Supernatural disappearances--Juvenile fiction. | Monsters--Juvenile fiction. | Graphic novels--Juvenile fiction. | Comic books, strips, etc.--Juvenile fiction.
Classification: DDC 741.5--dc23

Spotlight

A Division of ABDO
abdobooks.com

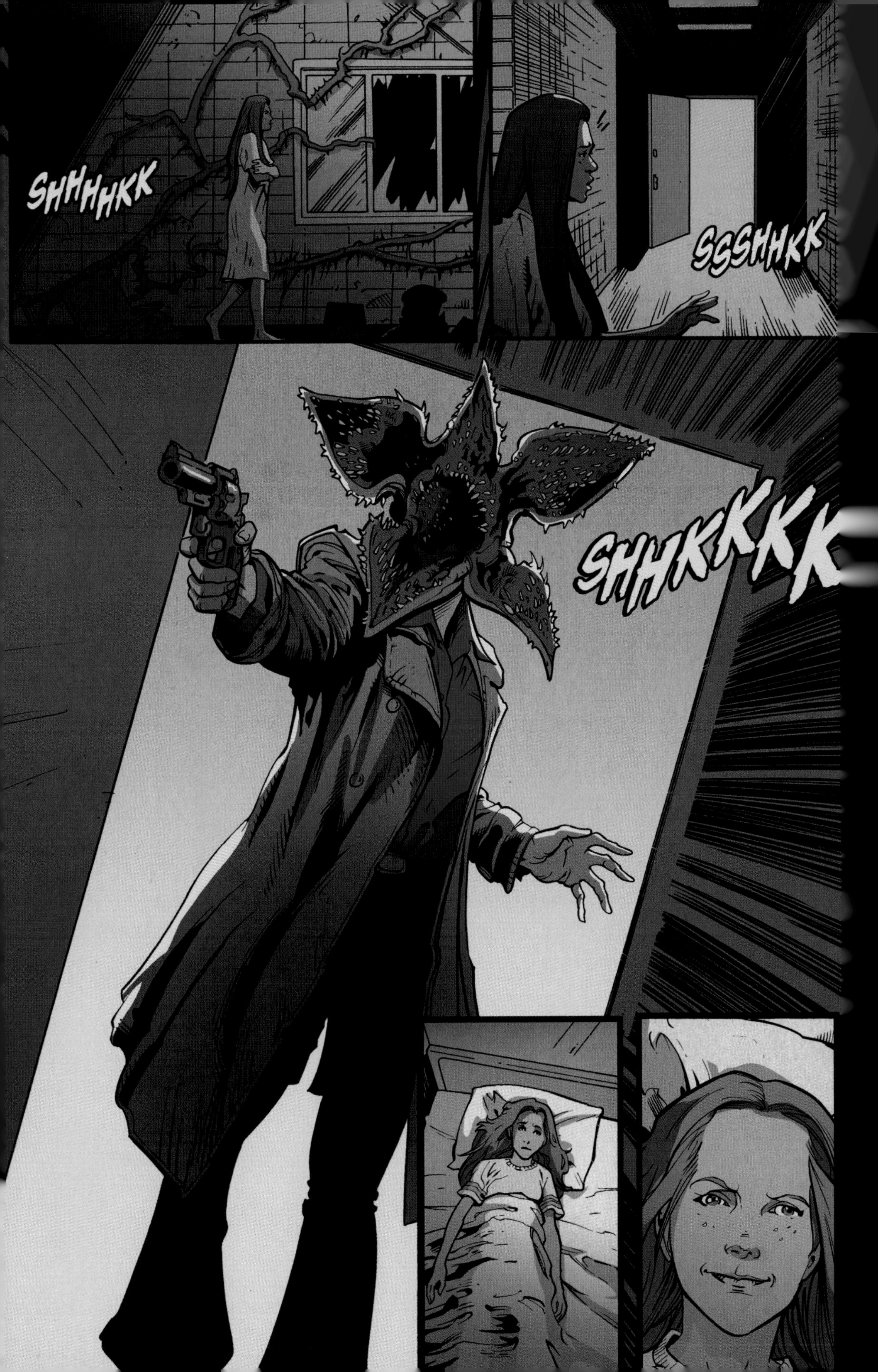
SHHHHKK
SSSHHKK
SHHKKKK

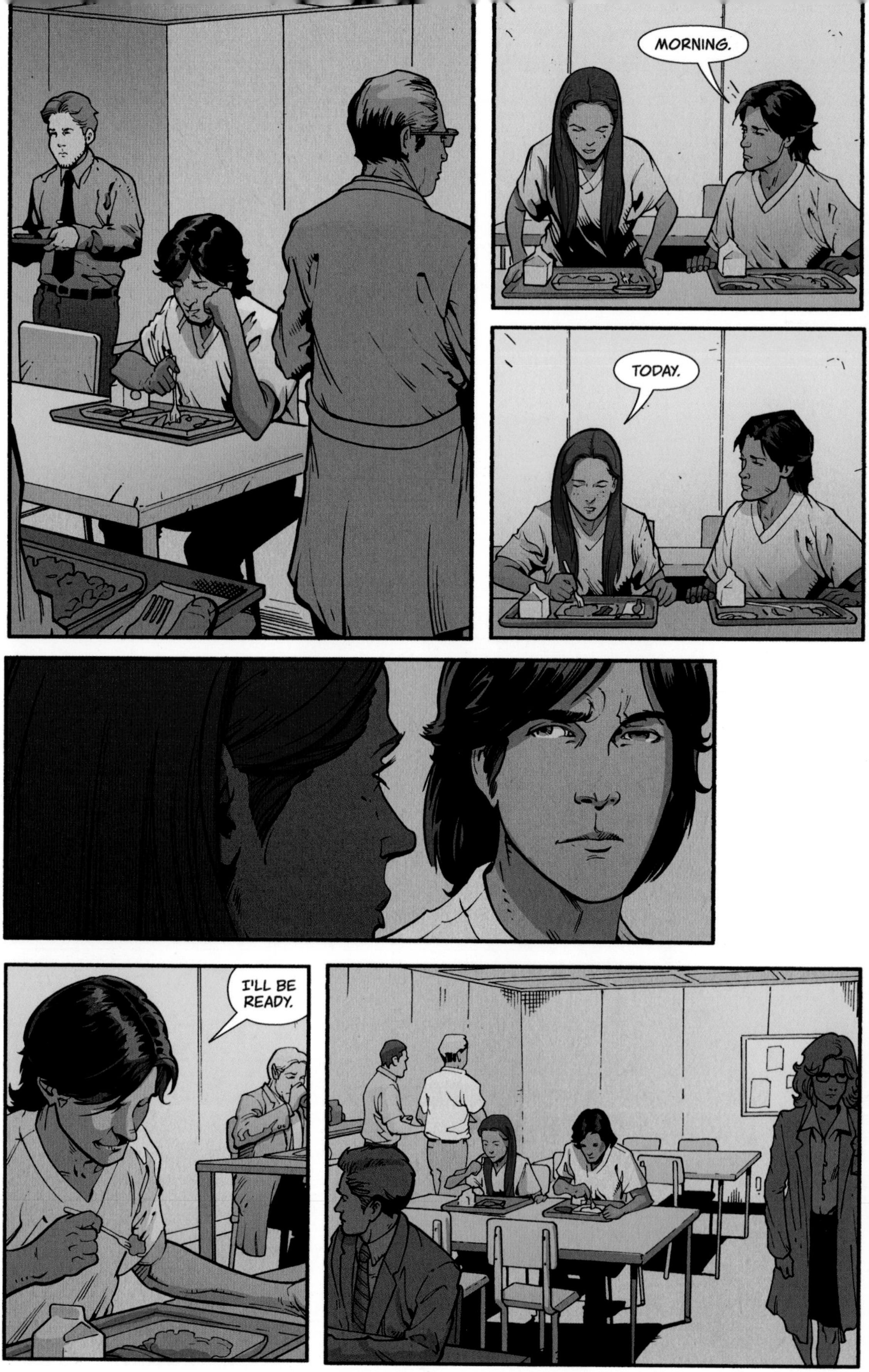
MORNING.
TODAY.
I'LL BE READY.

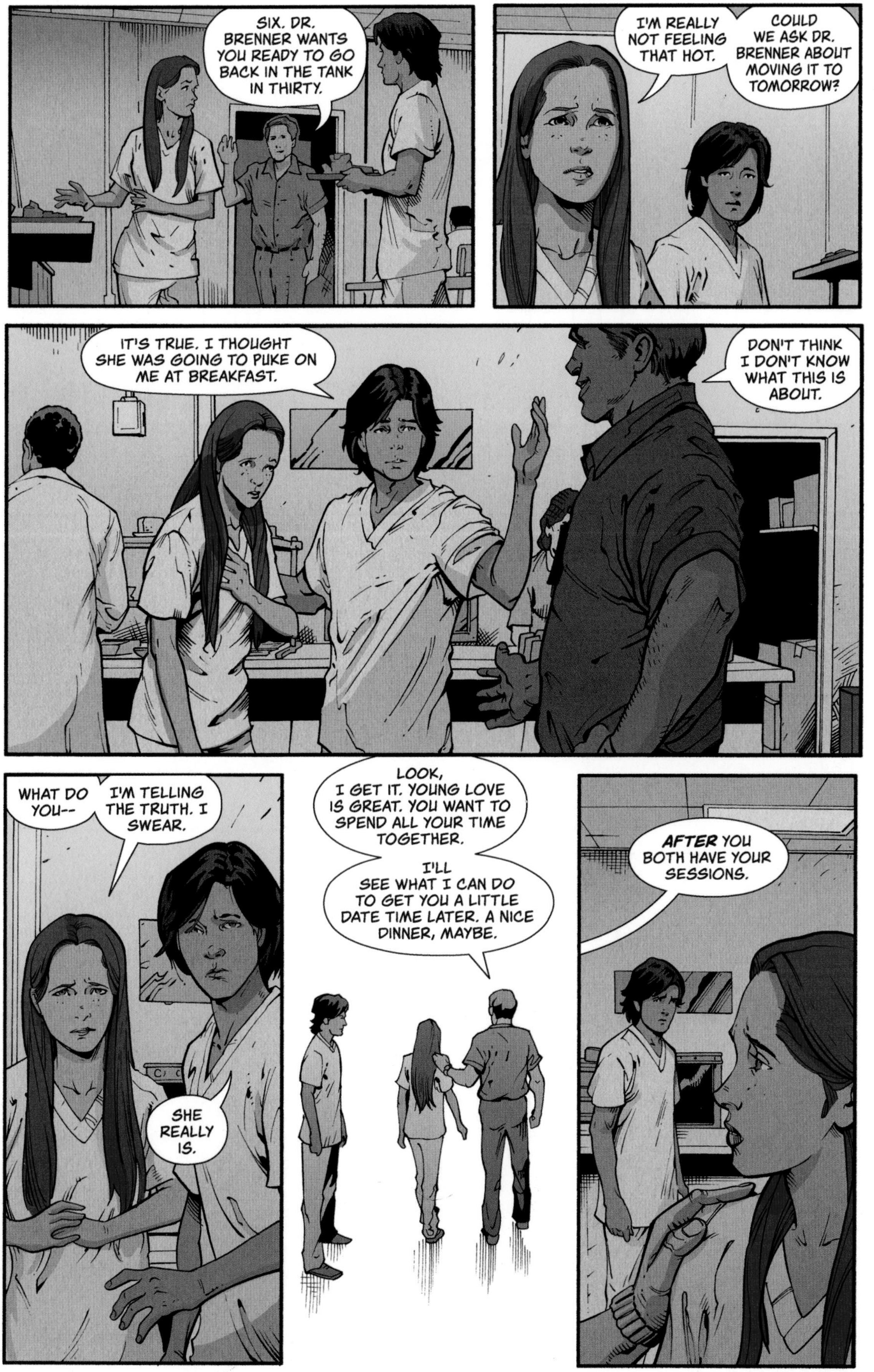
SIX. DR. BRENNER WANTS YOU READY TO GO BACK IN THE TANK IN THIRTY.
I'M REALLY NOT FEELING THAT HOT.
COULD WE ASK DR. BRENNER ABOUT MOVING IT TO TOMORROW?
IT'S TRUE. I THOUGHT SHE WAS GOING TO PUKE ON ME AT BREAKFAST.
DON'T THINK I DON'T KNOW WHAT THIS IS ABOUT.
WHAT DO YOU--
I'M TELLING THE TRUTH. I SWEAR.
SHE REALLY IS.
LOOK, I GET IT. YOUNG LOVE IS GREAT. YOU WANT TO SPEND ALL YOUR TIME TOGETHER.
I'LL SEE WHAT I CAN DO TO GET YOU A LITTLE DATE TIME LATER. A NICE DINNER, MAYBE.
AFTER YOU BOTH HAVE YOUR SESSIONS.

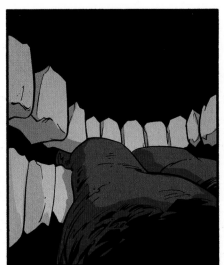

HEY, ARE YOU--

HURK! HURK!

OH NO!

I THINK SHE'S HAVING A SEIZURE!

I'LL GO GET BRENNER!

OW! STOP KICKING ME! I'M TRYING TO HELP HERE!

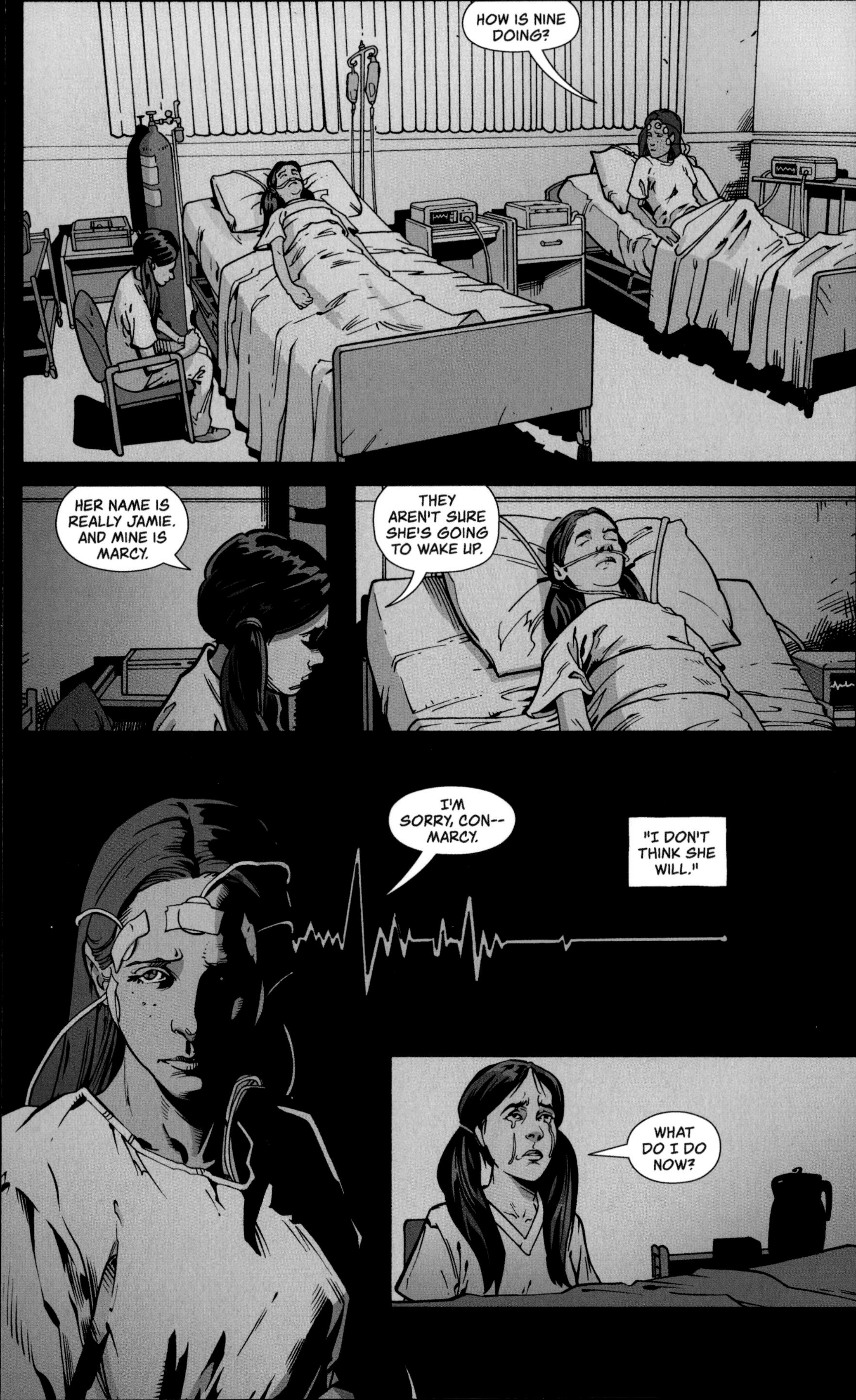
HOW IS NINE DOING?
HER NAME IS REALLY JAMIE. AND MINE IS MARCY.
THEY AREN'T SURE SHE'S GOING TO WAKE UP.
I'M SORRY, CON-- MARCY.
"I DON'T THINK SHE WILL."
WHAT DO I DO NOW?

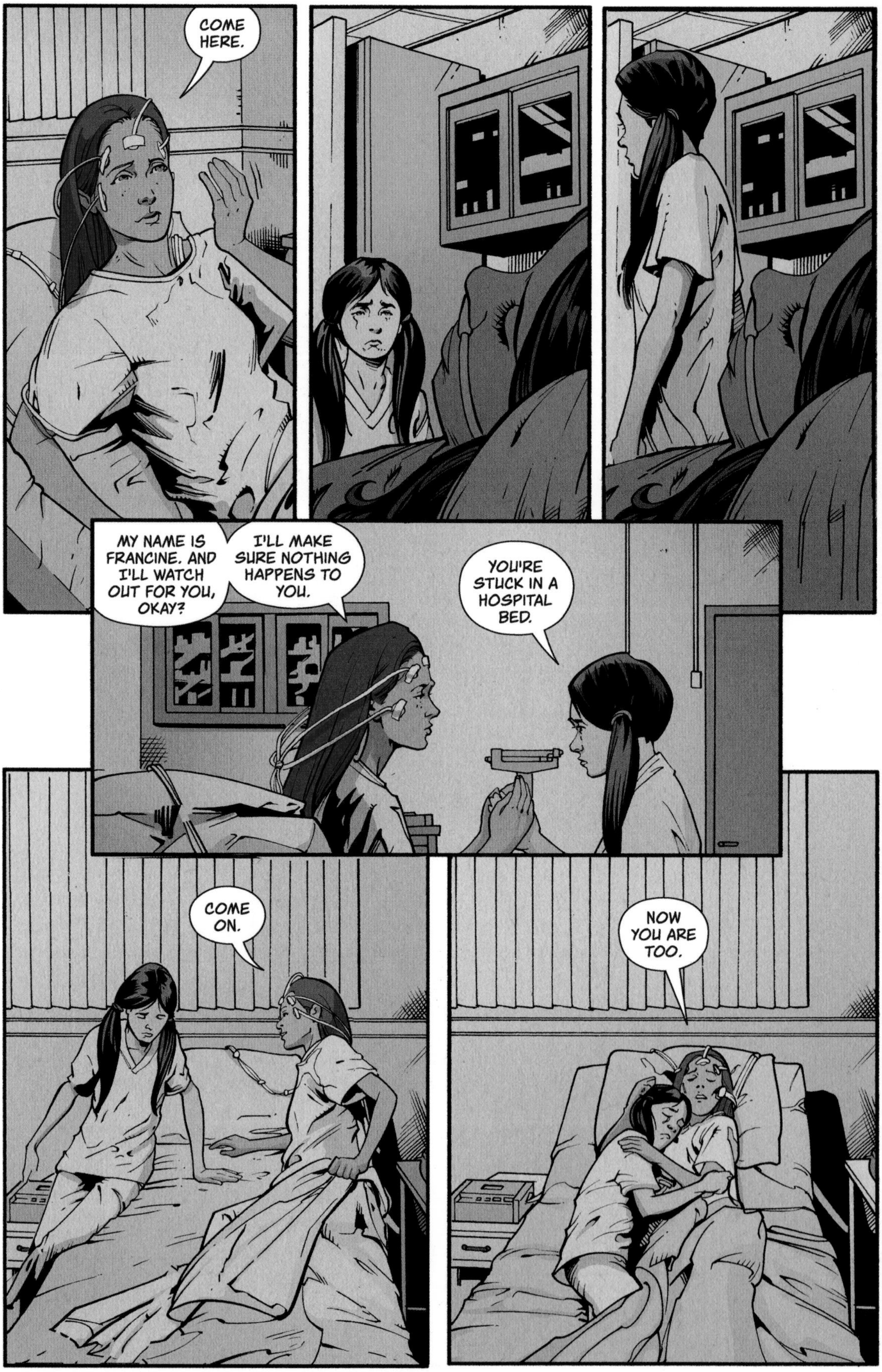
COME HERE.
MY NAME IS FRANCINE. AND I'LL WATCH OUT FOR YOU, OKAY?
I'LL MAKE SURE NOTHING HAPPENS TO YOU.
YOU'RE STUCK IN A HOSPITAL BED.
COME ON.
NOW YOU ARE TOO.

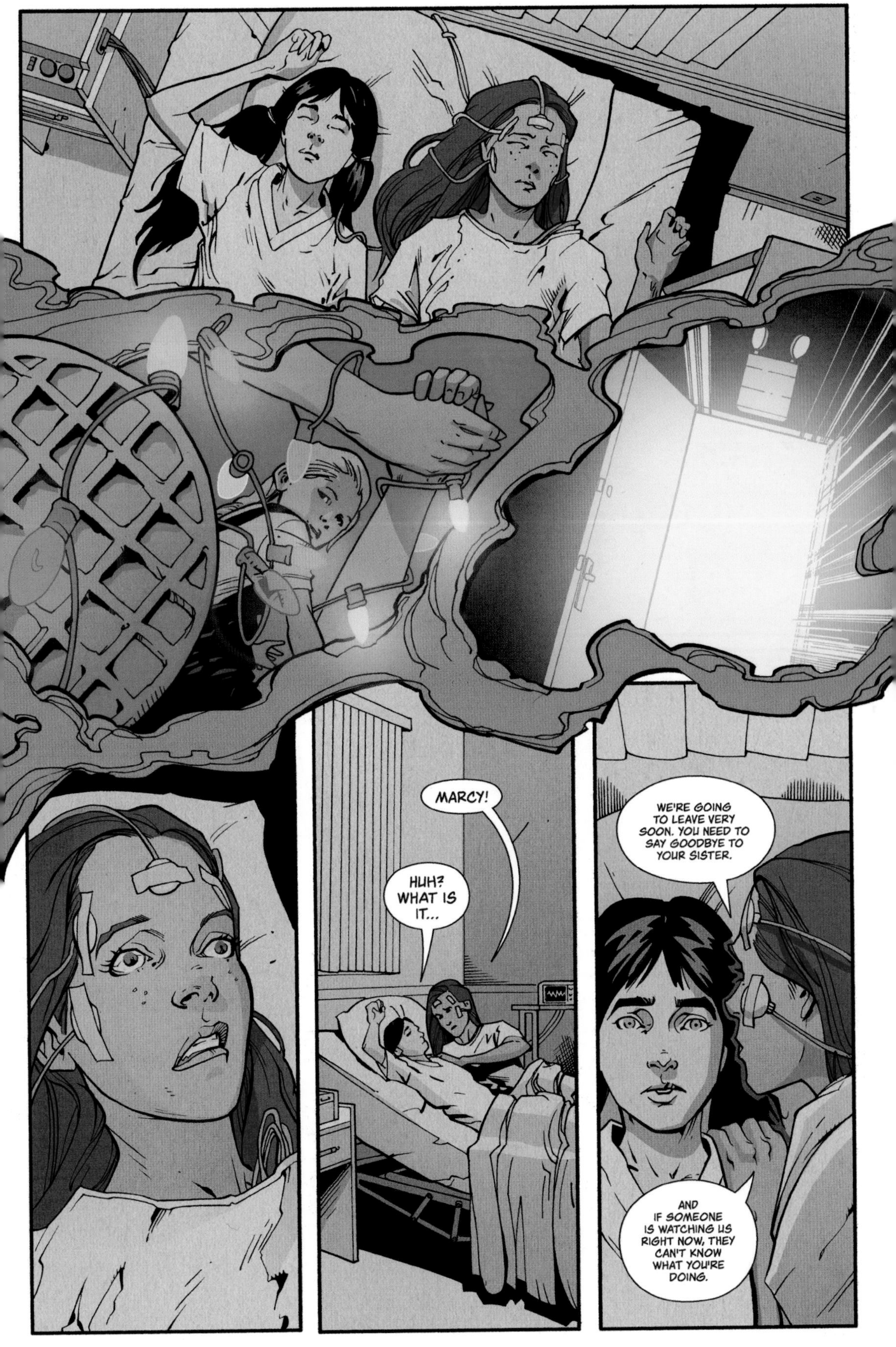
MARCY!
HUH? WHAT IS IT...
WE'RE GOING TO LEAVE VERY SOON. YOU NEED TO SAY GOODBYE TO YOUR SISTER.
AND IF SOMEONE IS WATCHING US RIGHT NOW, THEY CAN'T KNOW WHAT YOU'RE DOING.

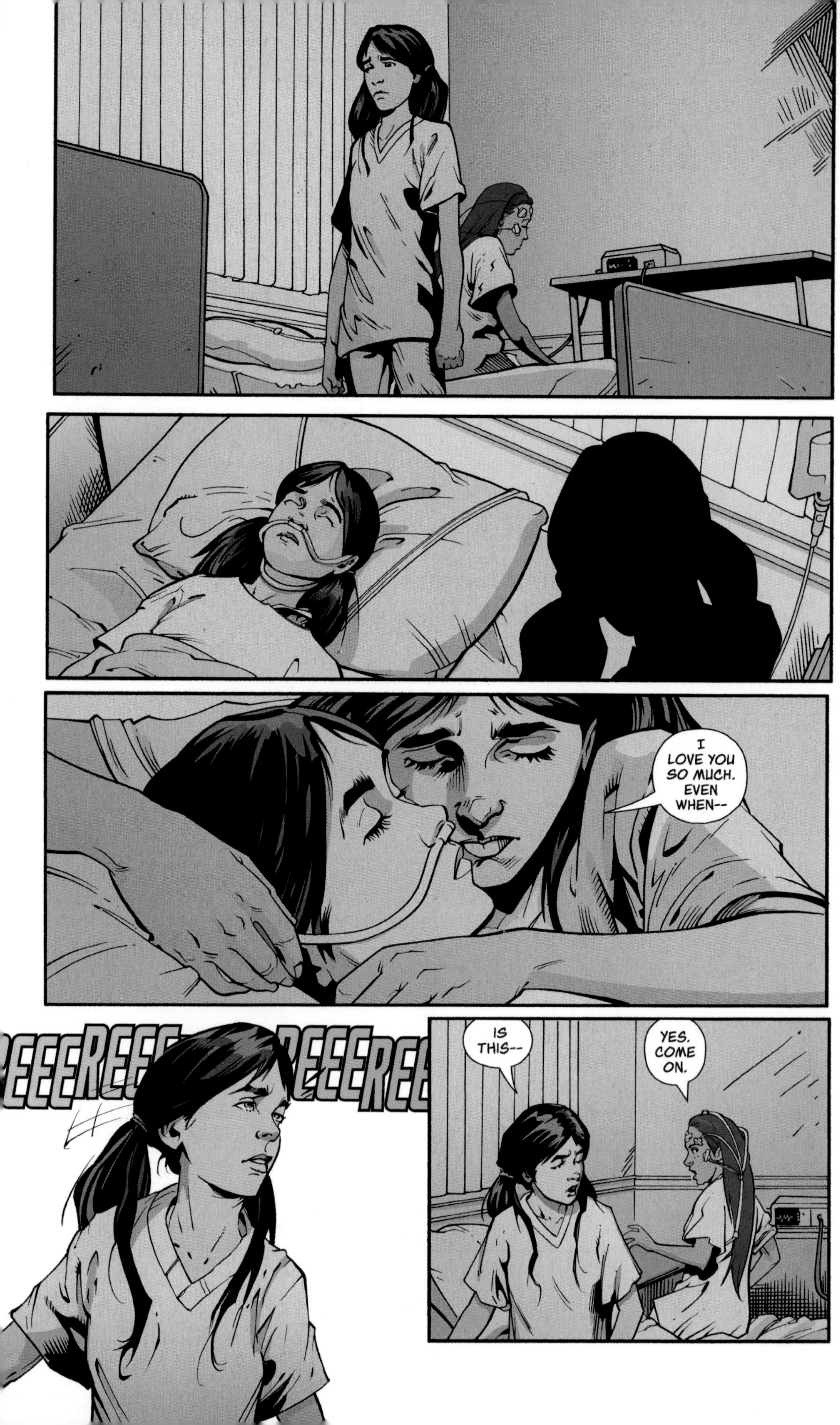

I LOVE YOU SO MUCH. EVEN WHEN--
REEEREEE
REEEREE
IS THIS--
YES. COME ON.

REEEREEEREE

REEEREEERE

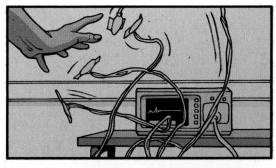

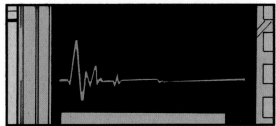

COME ON! WE HAVE TO FIND RICKY!

SIX? FRANCINE?

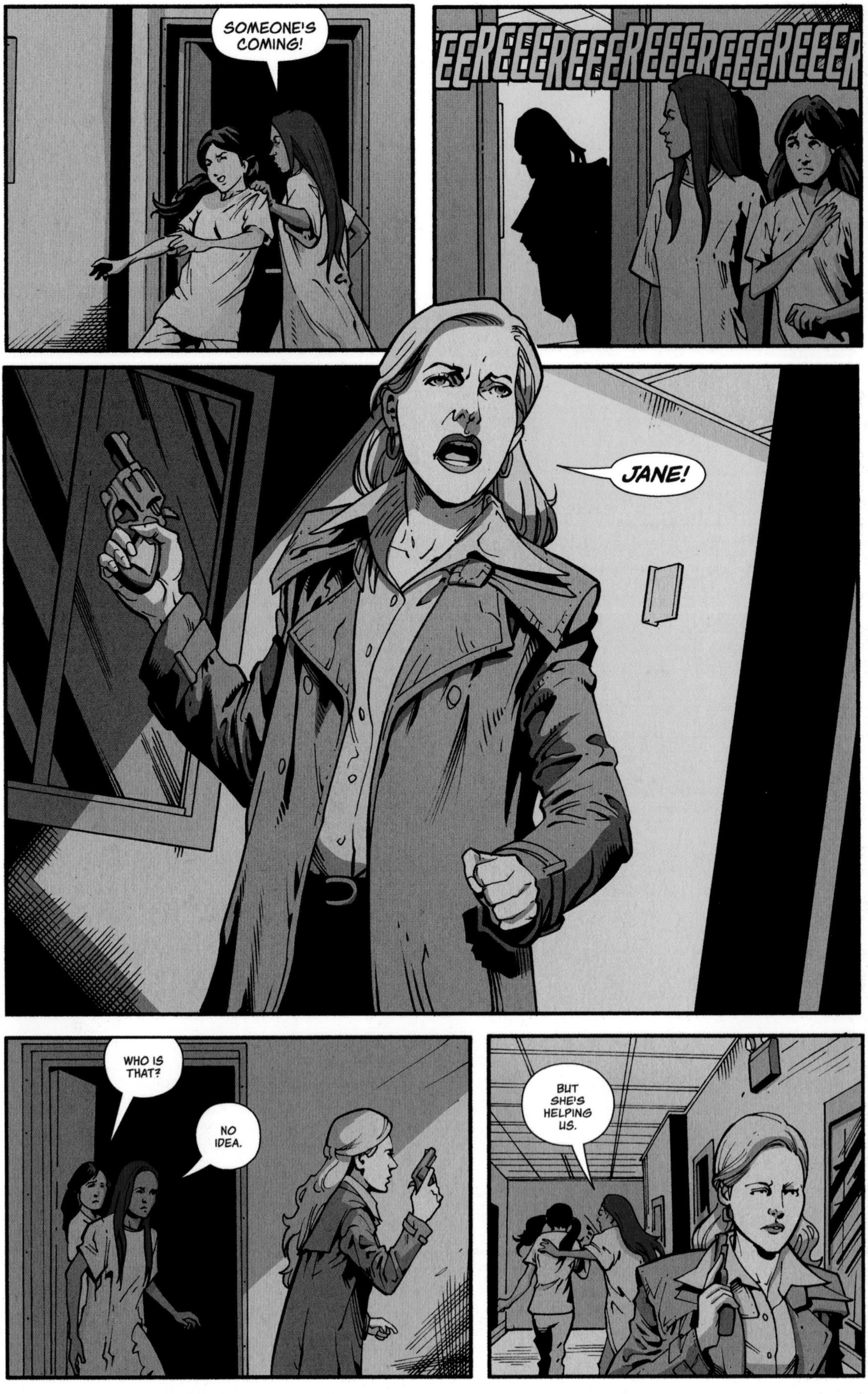
SOMEONE'S COMING!
EEREEEREEEREEEREEEREEER
JANE!
WHO IS THAT?
NO IDEA.
BUT SHE'S HELPING US.

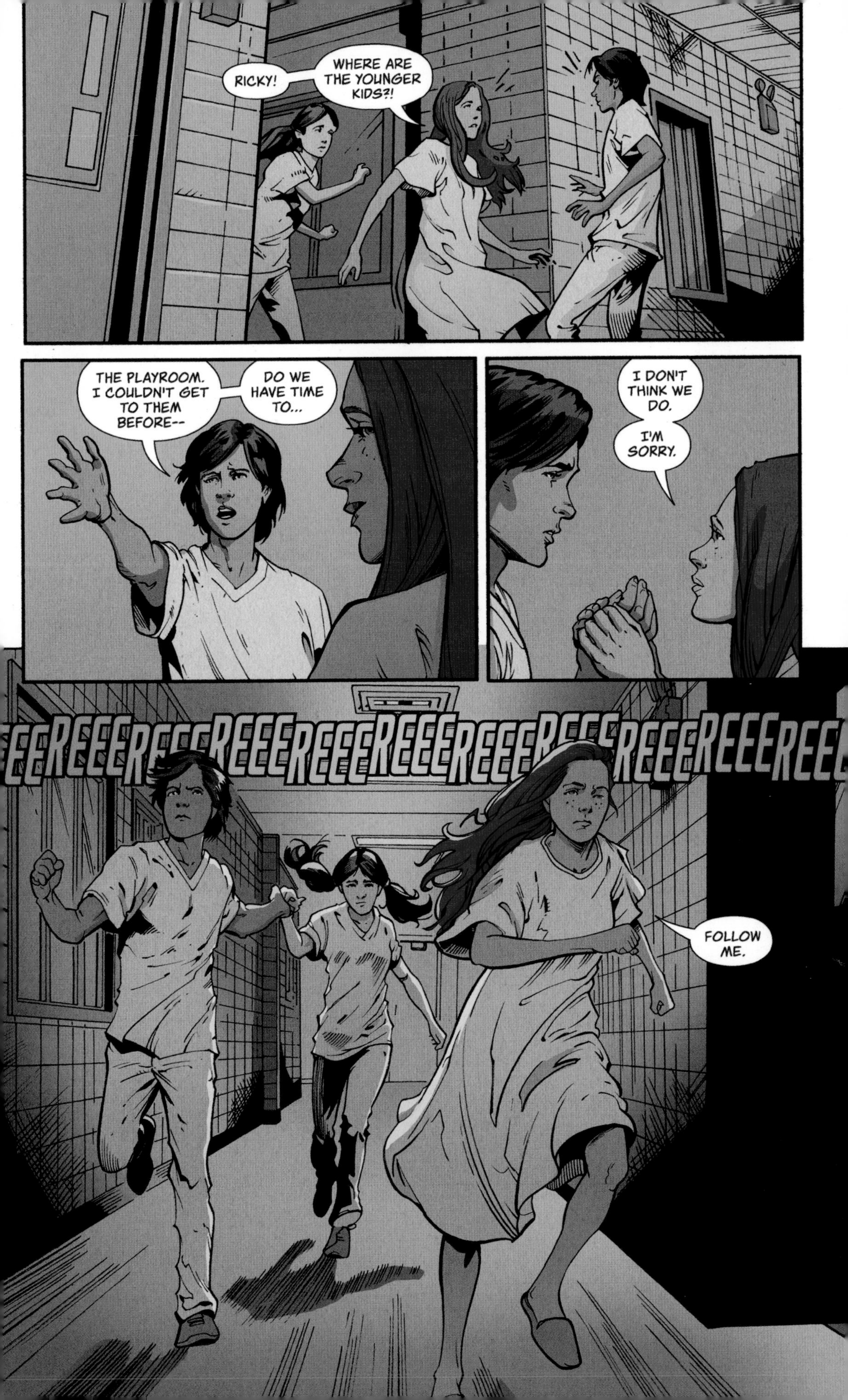
RICKY!
WHERE ARE THE YOUNGER KIDS?!
THE PLAYROOM. I COULDN'T GET TO THEM BEFORE--
DO WE HAVE TIME TO...
I DON'T THINK WE DO.
I'M SORRY.
EEREEEREEEREEEREEEREEEREEEREEEREEEREEEREEEREE
FOLLOW ME.

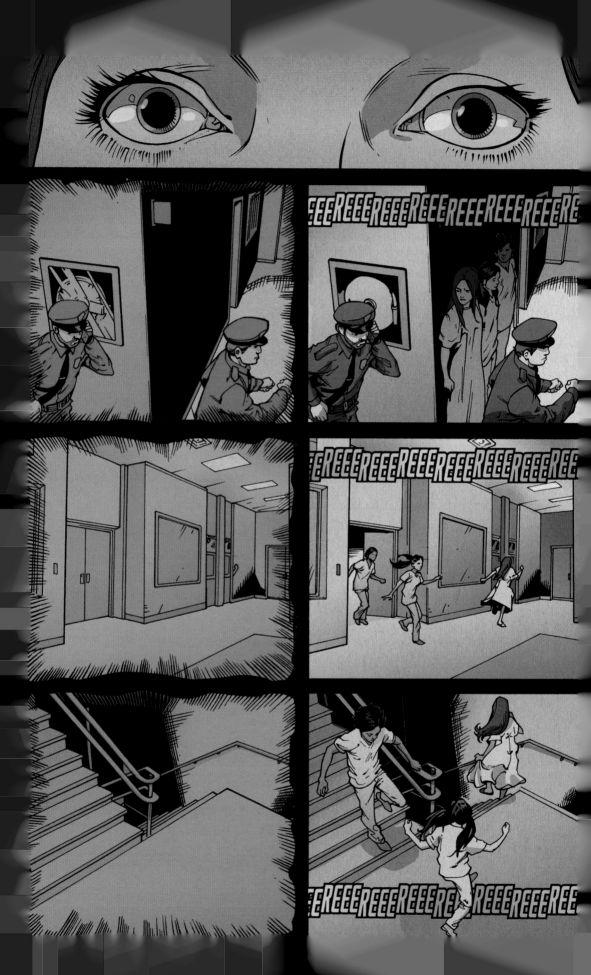

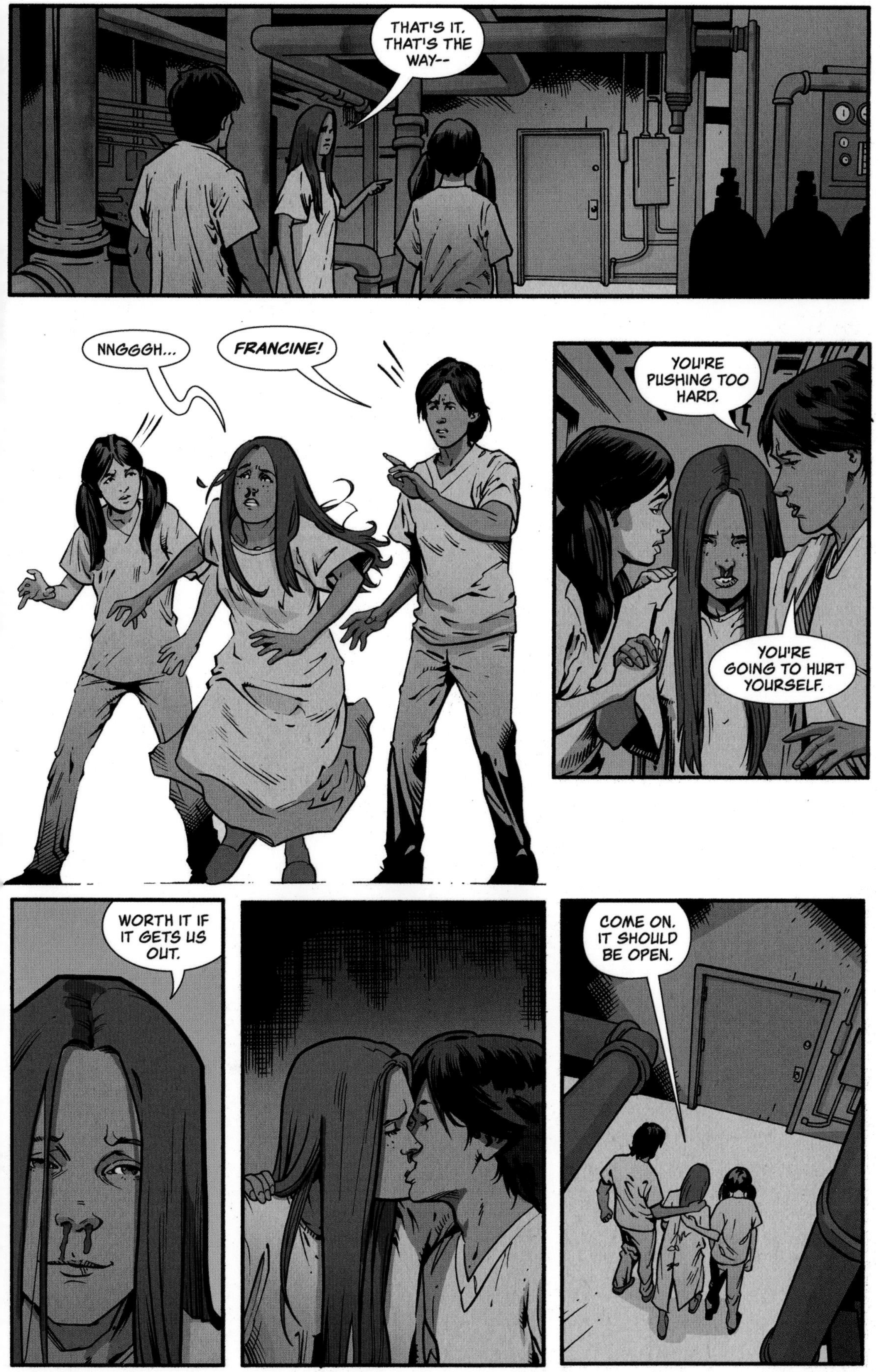
THAT'S IT. THAT'S THE WAY--
NNGGGH...
FRANCINE!
YOU'RE PUSHING TOO HARD.
YOU'RE GOING TO HURT YOURSELF.
WORTH IT IF IT GETS US OUT.
COME ON. IT SHOULD BE OPEN.

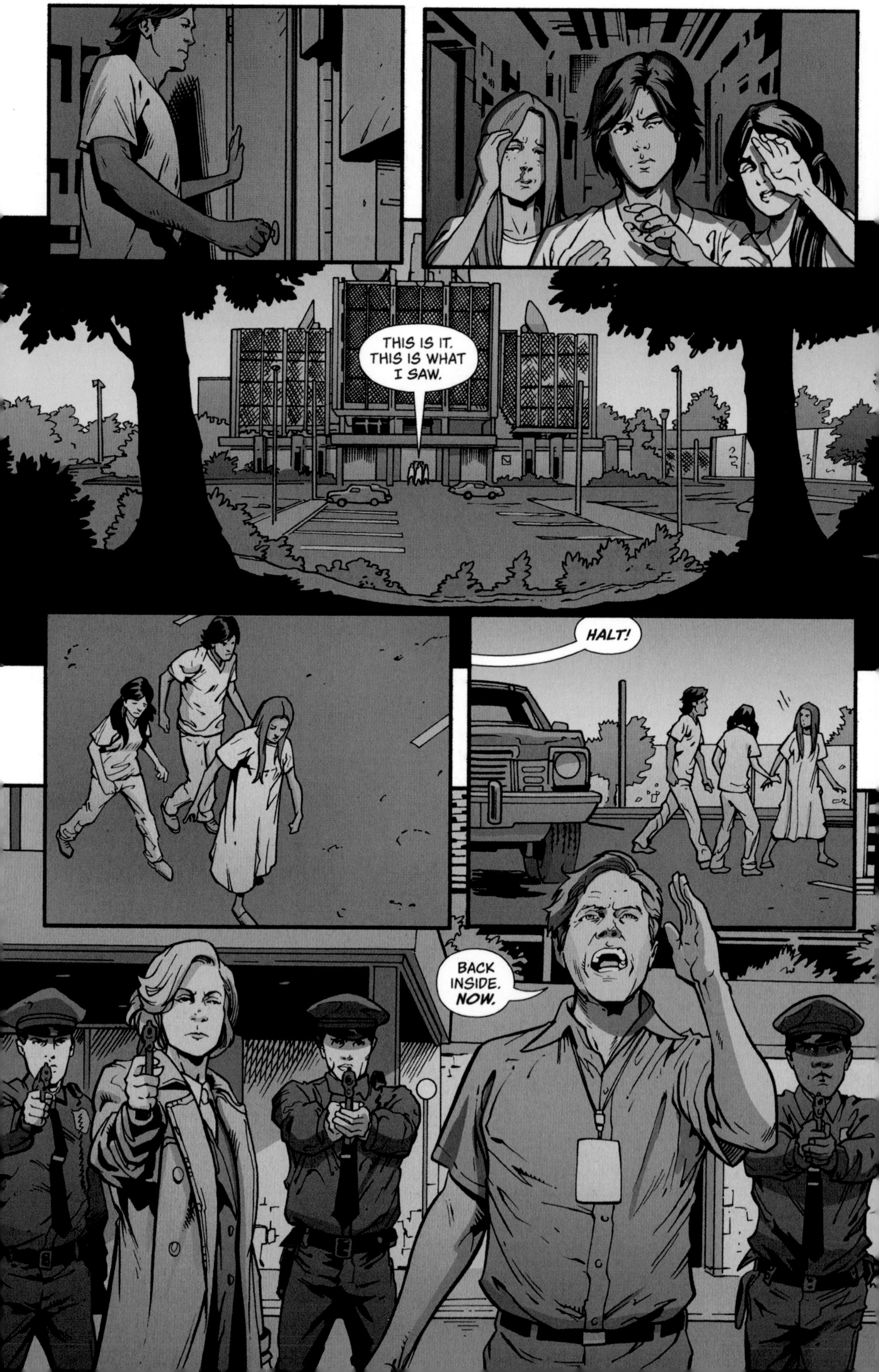
THIS IS IT. THIS IS WHAT I SAW.
HALT!
BACK INSIDE. NOW.

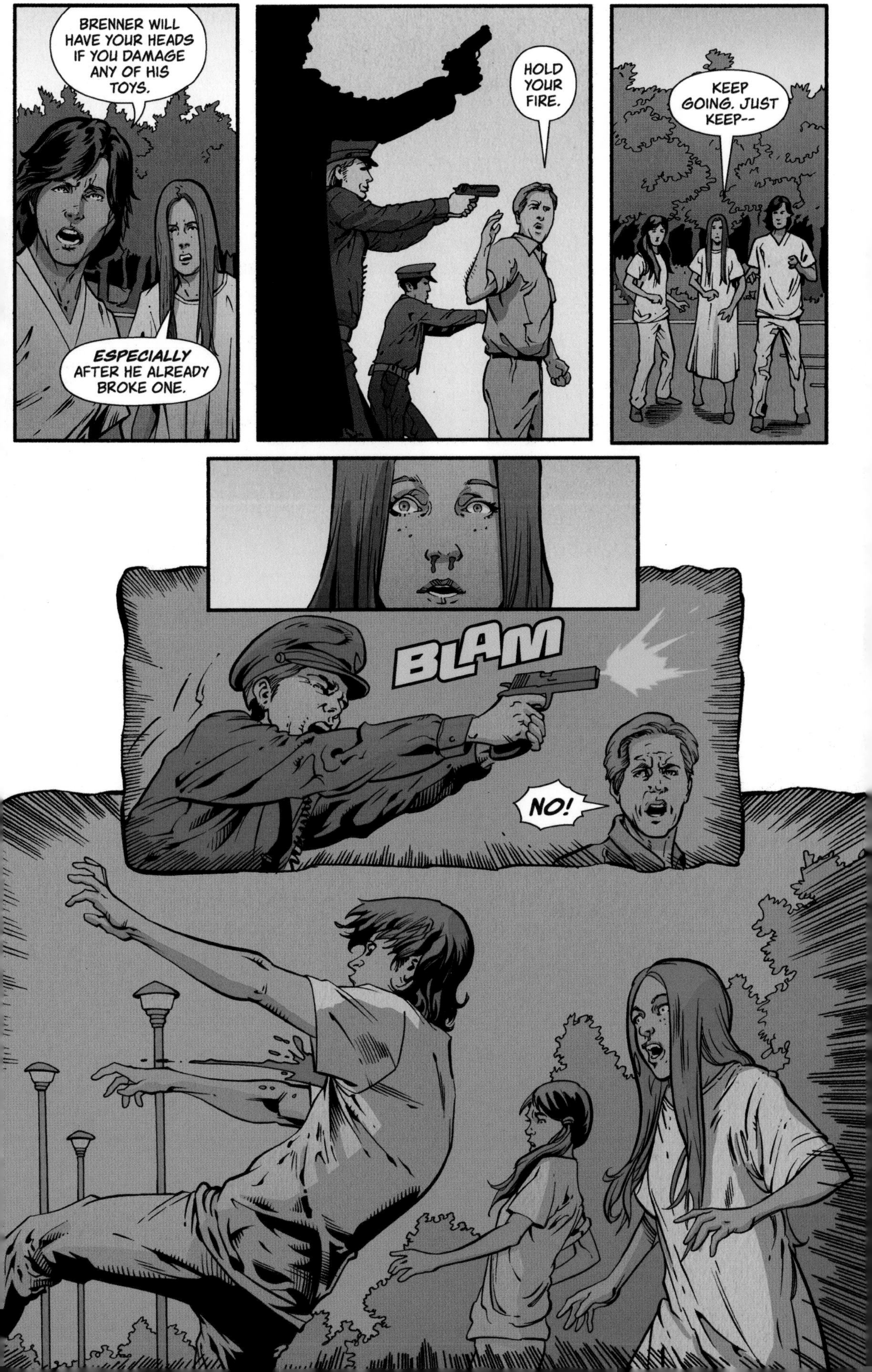
BRENNER WILL HAVE YOUR HEADS IF YOU DAMAGE ANY OF HIS TOYS.
ESPECIALLY AFTER HE ALREADY BROKE ONE.
HOLD YOUR FIRE.
KEEP GOING. JUST KEEP--
BLAM
NO!

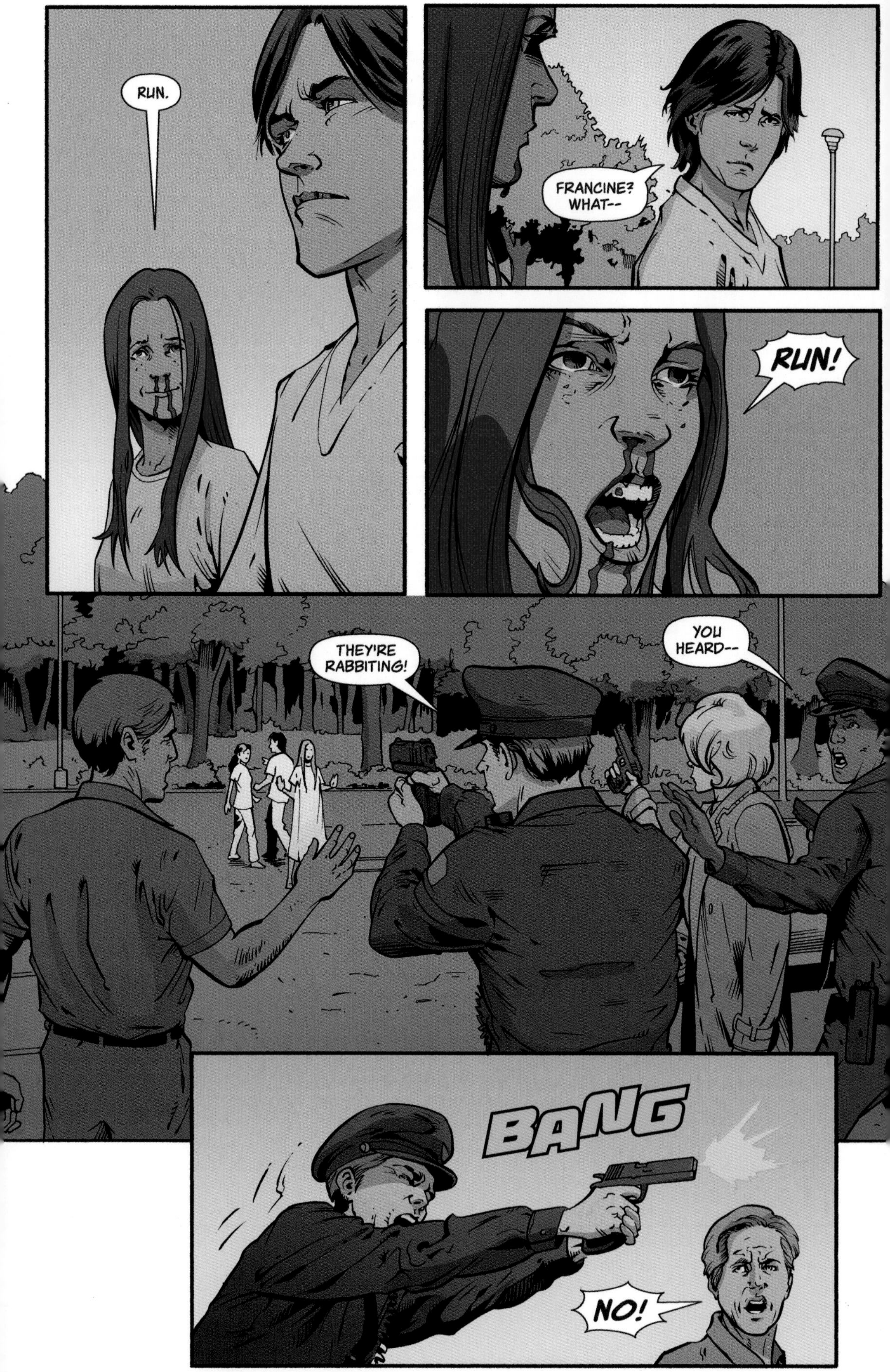
RUN.
FRANCINE? WHAT--
RUN!
THEY'RE RABBITING!
YOU HEARD--
BANG
NO!

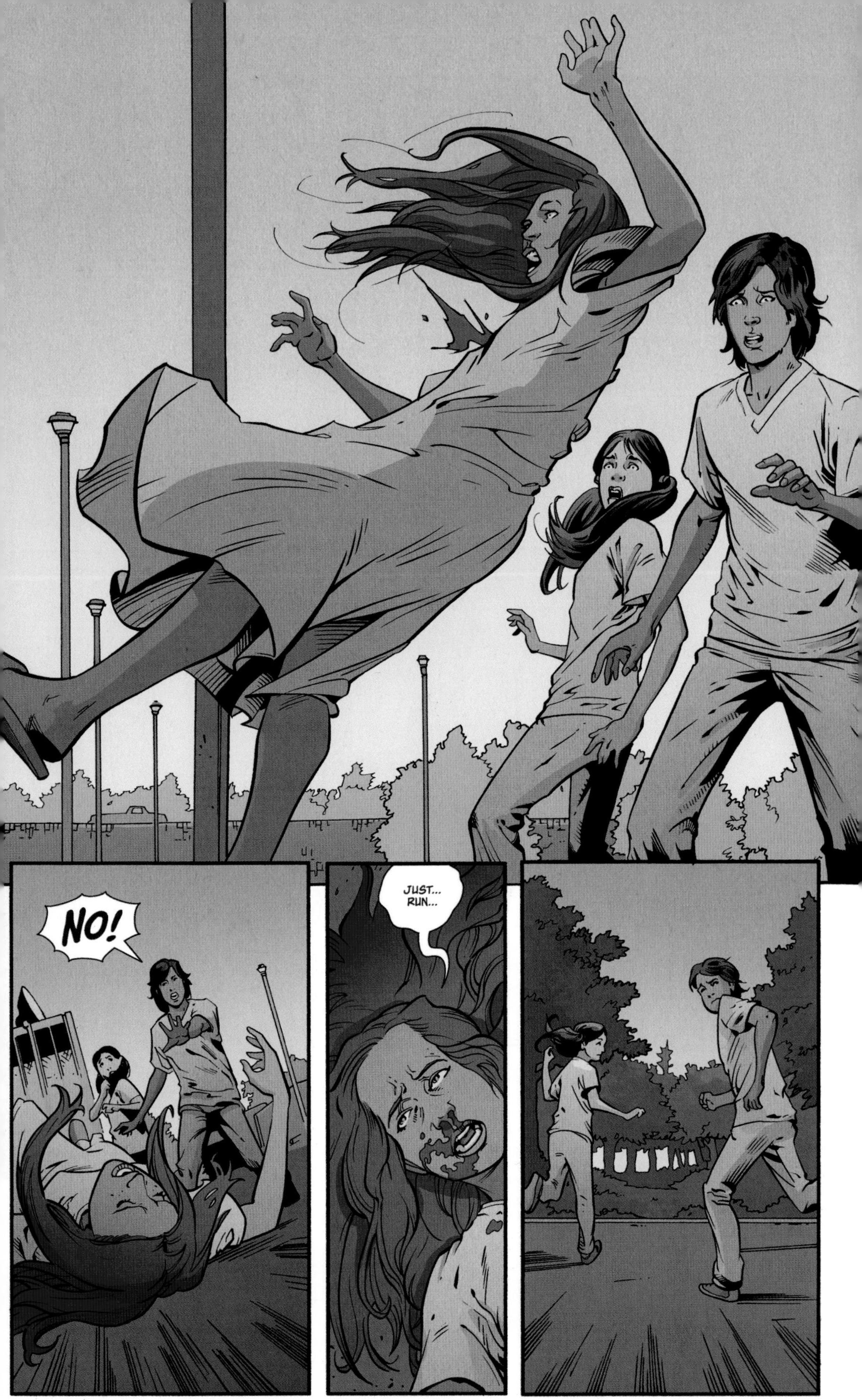
NO!
JUST... RUN...

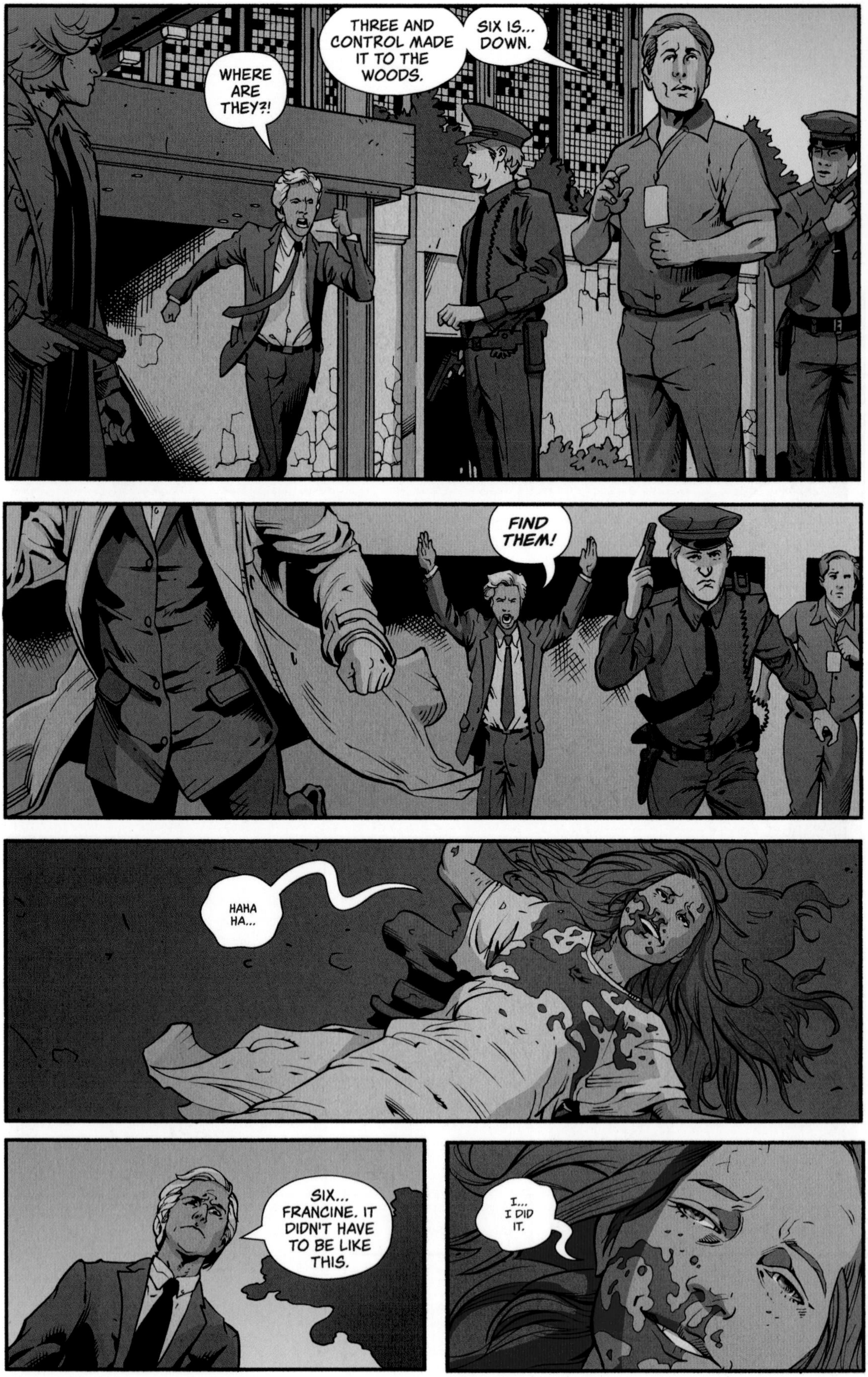
WHERE ARE THEY?!
THREE AND CONTROL MADE IT TO THE WOODS.
SIX IS... DOWN.
FIND THEM!
HAHA HA...
SIX... FRANCINE. IT DIDN'T HAVE TO BE LIKE THIS.
I... I DID IT.

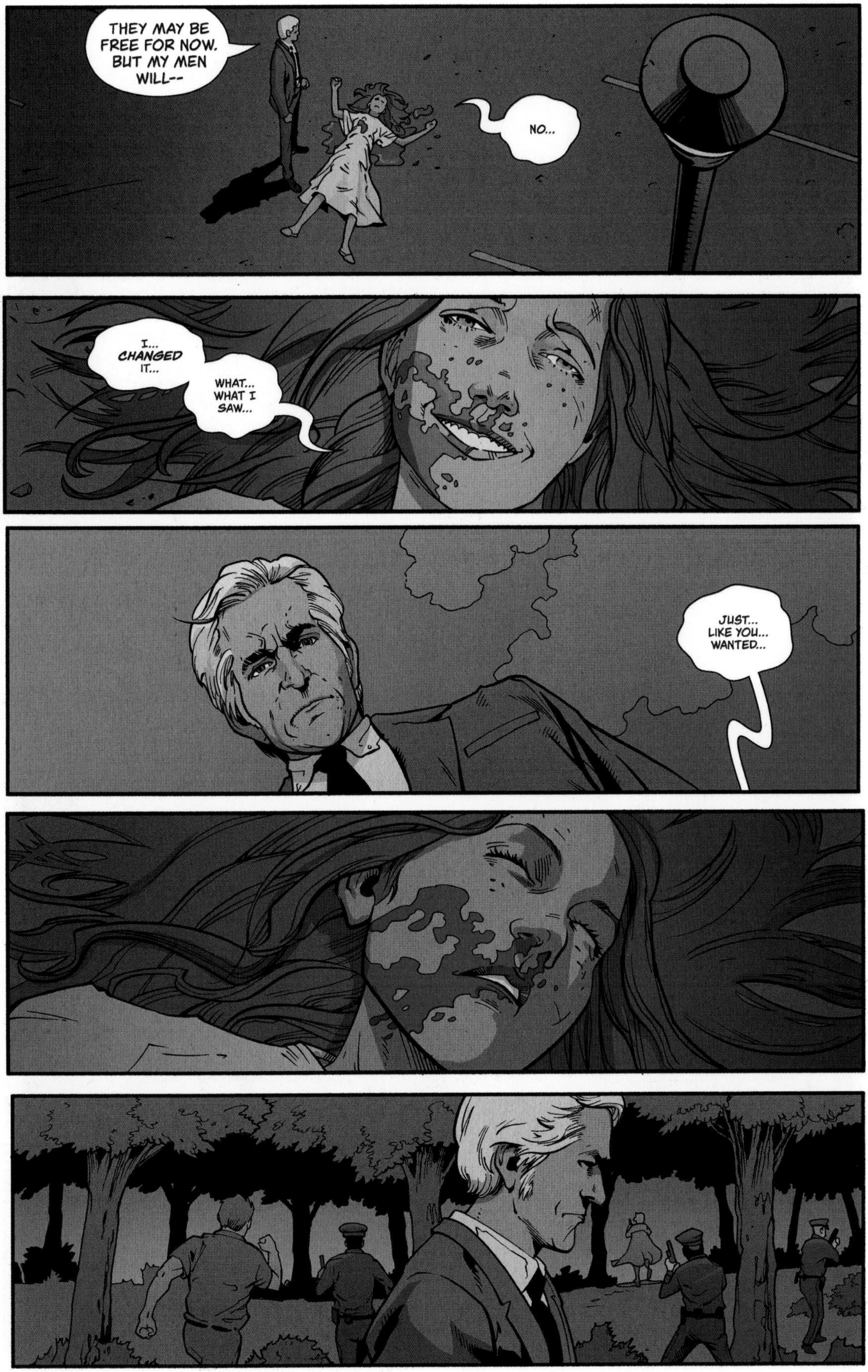
THEY MAY BE FREE FOR NOW. BUT MY MEN WILL--
NO...
I... CHANGED IT...
WHAT... WHAT I SAW...
JUST... LIKE YOU... WANTED...

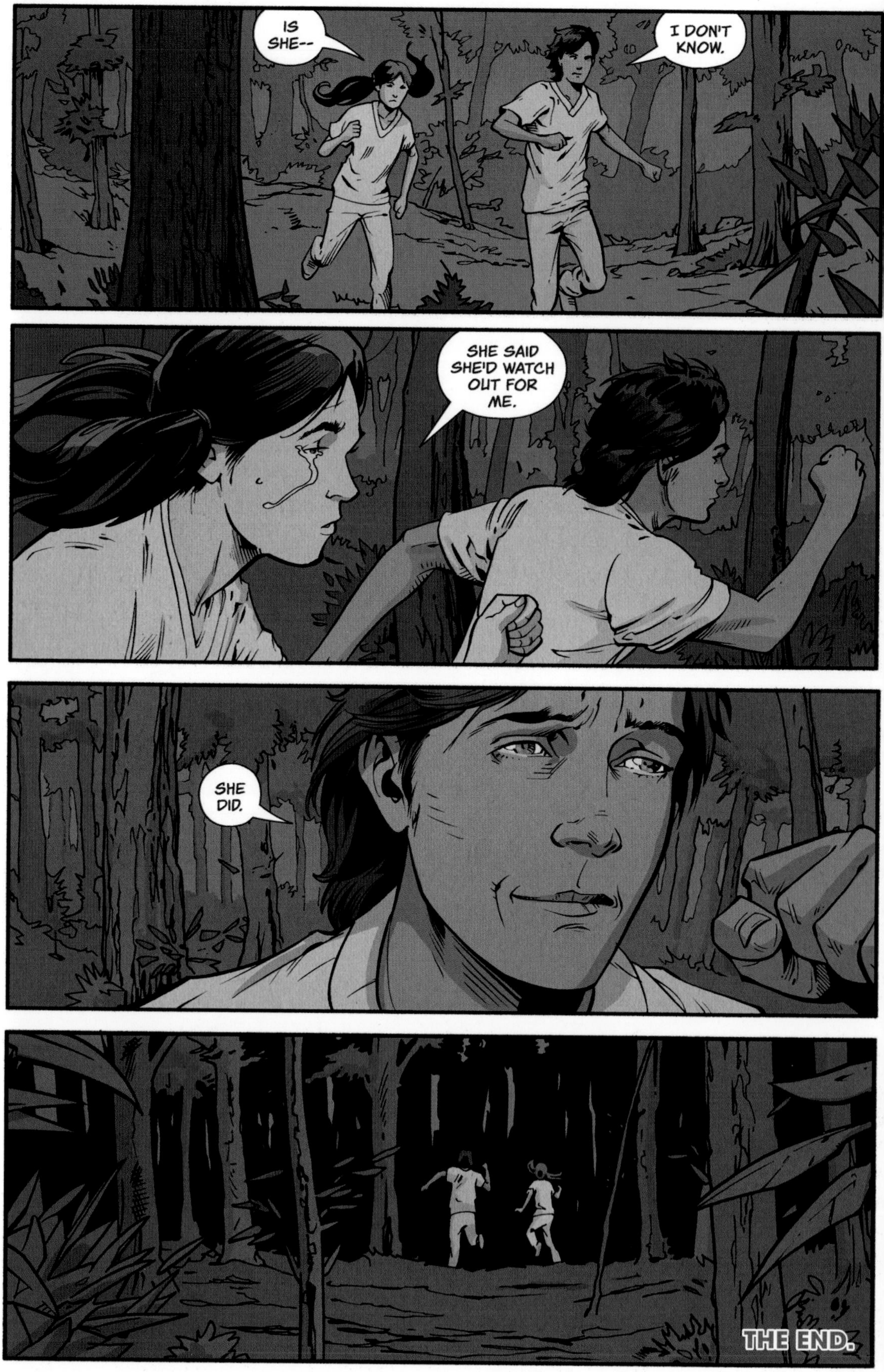
IS SHE--
I DON'T KNOW.
SHE SAID SHE'D WATCH OUT FOR ME.
SHE DID.
THE END.